Oh, What a Mess

Oh, What a Mess

Hans Wilhelm

Crown Publishers, Inc., New York

To Stephane

Published by Crown Publishers, Inc. 225 Park Avenue South, New York, New York 10003 and
represented in Canada by the Canadian MANDA Group
CROWN is a trademark of Crown Publishers, Inc.
Manufactured in Hong Kong.
Library of Congress Cataloging-in-Publication Data
Wilhelm, Hans, 1945–
   Oh what a mess/by Hans Wilhelm.
   Summary: After Franklin Pig wins first prize in an art contest,
his very messy family finally begins to put their home in order.
[1. Pigs—Fiction.   2. Orderliness—Fiction.]   I. Title.
PZ7.W648160h   1988
[E]—dc19   87-30507 CIP AC

ISBN: 0-517-56909-4

10 9 8 7 6 5 4 3 2 1

First Edition

Most of the time Franklin was alone. He would have liked some friends but he never invited anyone home. Why?

The truth is, Franklin was too embarrassed. His family was very lazy and very messy. They never, ever cleaned up. They didn't sweep, wash dishes, or make their beds. They only took baths once a year—and then only if it was absolutely necessary!

The house was so messy it was even dangerous to walk around. Franklin was always slipping on toys that hadn't been put away. Someone in the family was always sick or hurt. Franklin's parents didn't seem to care very much. They spent most of their time sleeping.

Every morning Franklin got up early for school. His brothers always overslept. Then at the last minute they would wake up and follow Franklin to school—without washing up or eating breakfast.

At school the teacher made Franklin's brothers sit apart from the other students. They were simply too dirty and smelly—even for pigs. Franklin often wished his brothers would change a little, but his brothers didn't seem to care.

One day all the pigs had to paint a picture. They could paint whatever they liked. Franklin decided to paint a pretty rainbow. He worked hard at it.

When it was finished Franklin's rainbow was the most beautiful painting in the whole class. The teacher held it up for everyone to see, and then she pinned a beautiful ribbon on it—first prize!

Franklin wasn't used to this kind of attention. He was a little shy. "It really is not th-a-t good," he tried to apologize. But deep down he was happy to have won the honor.

"I wonder what my parents will say," he thought as he carried his picture home.

To Franklin's delight,
his family was impressed.

"Look at this! We've got a real Rembrandt in our family!" cried his father with pride.

"This is the loveliest rainbow I have ever seen!" added Franklin's mother.

Grandfather nodded and quietly said that this picture was a true masterpiece.

"Hang it up on the wall over there!" demanded his father.

"Oh, I don't know..." Franklin tried to say. But his father insisted. "Don't be shy, son. This picture deserves to be seen by everyone!"

When the picture was on the wall Franklin stepped back. "Do you think," he said quietly, "it would look nicer if the wall was a bit cleaner?"

"Maybe so, son," Father said. "Maybe you are right. Let's give it a try and wash the wall."

And Franklin's father began to scrub the
dirty wall with lots of soap and water.

"Look!" he noticed. "There is wallpaper
underneath!"

"And what a pretty design!" added Franklin's
mother.

After the job was done Franklin said, "Thank you for cleaning the wall. The picture really looks much better now."

"Well, such a fine painting deserves a fine place to hang! But now that the wall is clean, it's a shame the floor is so messy. Maybe we should do something about this old straw."

"Here, let me do it," interrupted
Grandfather. "I had intended to change this
old straw for the last fifty years but I never
got around to it. Now I have a good reason
to get started."

And he cleaned out all the old straw and
put down fresh new straw everywhere.

After that the whole family agreed that the prize-winning painting looked even better in its shiny clean surroundings.

"But the curtains!" said Franklin's mother. "We nearly forgot the curtains. We can't leave them dirty. I must wash them, too." So she took them down from the windows and carried them outside to wash them in the trough.

Washing those curtains took a lot of soap and water. A lovely soft white foam rose from the trough and spilled bubbles over the sides.

It looked so tempting that suddenly the whole family jumped in for a bubble bath!

They spent the whole afternoon in the trough, splashing and playing, grunting and laughing.

Franklin began to feel much better about his family. Soon he even invited some of his schoolmates to come over. His mother served them cookies and his father found an old harmonica and began to play songs.

Grandfather joined in a few games, too.
Before they left, Franklin's friends told him,
"Your family is the best!" Franklin had to agree.

From then on, life was much happier for Franklin and his family. With his parents' encouragement, Franklin took painting lessons and his talent blossomed. His mother, his father, his grandfather, even his brothers managed to keep the house—and themselves—clean and neat.

Only once in a while they
all took a crazy mud bath
together—including Franklin!